CONDUCTOR OF HEARTS
FILTHY RICH LOVE

SADIE KING

LET'S BE BESTIES!

A few times a month I send out an email with new releases, special deals and sneak peeks of what I'm working on. If you want to get on the list I'd love to meet you!

When you join you'll get access to all my bonus content which includes a couple of free short and steamy romances plus bonus scenes for selected books.

Sign up here:
authorsadieking.com/bonus-scenes

CONDUCTOR OF HEARTS

A curvy delivery girl with a talent and an older billionaire whose passion could be her undoing...

Ayden

I return home after years of travelling the world, but I'm restless and ready to move on. Then I find Laila sitting at my piano.

Her music fills my empty house, lifts my soul, and sets my body on fire. I'll do just about anything to keep her playing, and I'm beginning to realize some things are worth sticking around for.

Laila

I've worked hard to get an audition at a prestigious music school. But with two days to go I meet Ayden.

Now my head's spinning, my body's in a fever, and I'm stumbling over the notes.

Can I pull it together for the audition, or will this gorgeous, globe-trotting entrepreneur be my downfall?

Conductor of Hearts is a short and steamy age gap billionaire romance featuring an older man and a younger innocent woman.

Copyright © 2019 by Sadie King.

All rights reserved.

No part of this book may be reproduced in any form or by any electronic or mechanical means, including information storage and retrieval systems, without written permission from the author, except for the use of brief quotations in a book review.

Cover designed by Cormer Covers.

This is a work of fiction. Any resemblance to actual events, companies, locales or persons living or dead, are entirely coincidental.

www.authorsadieking.com

1
LAILA

Tap tap tappity-tap. Two notes with the pinky and down to the lower G.

My thumb slides off the steering wheel as I turn into the wide driveway. Three days away from the most important audition of my life and instead of practicing at home like all the other Sunset Coast Music School hopefuls, I'm stuck in a white van delivering packages around the outer reaches of Cod Cove.

"Oh, wow." The house comes into view, and I catch my breath. It's a Georgian-style mansion, its white stonework glinting in the sun. A balcony runs around the second floor and rose vines have grown between the banisters, adding splashes of bright color. It's beautiful.

The tires crunch on the pebbles as I pull up next to a black Porsche convertible. Whoever lives here has fantastic taste in cars.

I get out of the van and stand for a moment admiring the house. A warm tingle spreads up my neck. Despite its size there's a lovely feel about this place, inviting and warm.

I wonder if there's some old-fashioned servants' entrance I'm supposed to use. I dismiss the idea. The wide stone steps and grand pillars are too inviting not to use. It makes an elegant change from the crumbling condos I mostly deliver to. I grab my scanner and the package out of the back and head up the front steps.

The door is open a crack, and I catch a glimpse of shiny white marble flooring and what could be the start of a spiral staircase. I resist the urge to push it open further and have a good look around and instead ring the buzzer.

The noise echoes throughout the house, but there's no sound from inside. I push it again and drum my fingers on my thighs, moving through the trickiest part of my audition piece while I wait.

I get stuck again at the start of the crescendo. It doesn't feel right jumping to the G. I need to hear it to check that I've got it right. But I've still got half a van of deliveries to make before I can get home and get to my piano. Some of the keys get stuck and it needs tuning almost daily, but the old girl has got me this far and she's all I've got.

I ring the doorbell again impatiently. In my haste, I bump the door open a little more.

"Hello?" My voice echoes back to me through the enormous entry hall. "Signed delivery."

There's a large gilt-framed mirror hanging on the wall, and I see a spiral staircase reflected in it. It's beautiful, and I so desperately want to get a better look.

You're not supposed to go into the houses, but the door *is* open, and no one answered the bell, so . . .? I edge it open just a bit further and take a tentative step across the threshold.

"I've got a delivery for Mr. Miller."

Holy cow, there's a Steinway baby grand in the entryway nestled under the curve of the staircase. My fingers itch at the sight of it. The lid is propped up open and ready as if someone's just stepped away.

The keys are calling to me, and before I know what I'm doing I'm inside the house and in front of the piano. I can't seem to stop myself. I leave the package and my scanner on the floor and sit down on the plush velvet stool.

I glance around guiltily, but there's no one here. They must be in the garden or something if they didn't hear the bell and didn't hear me call. Surely it won't hurt to have a little play just to get this tricky part fixed in my head.

I brush my fingers over the keys. They're smooth as silk, and I bet they don't stick like the ones at home sometimes do. I run through the C Major scale. The acoustics of the entryway give it a clear, vibrant sound.

When I finish the grand entrance hall returns to silence. No one runs down the stair to tell me off, there's no sound of footsteps. Whoever lives here can't hear me. It will only take a few minutes to play the piece.

I take a deep breath and start to play.

The notes sing out in the entryway; the high ceiling and hollow space make for an excellent chamber hall. The music spirals up the staircase and fills the room.

The tapping I've been doing all day is released in these notes, the tingling starting in my fingertips and spreading through my body until I'm unaware of anything else around me. My body is taut, all my concentration focused on my fingertips as they dance over the notes. My hands fly over the keys, and my heart soars. It's the release I've been waiting for.

I'm coming up to the difficult bit and I tell my mind to relax, to stay in the moment. But already I'm slowing down, my fingers are fumbling, and I'm having to think about the notes rather than play them automatically.

Sweat beads on my forehead and my heart races as I reach the crescendo. I'm doing it, I'm doing it!

Damn! My finger slips, and I miss a note. Most people wouldn't notice, but it rings out like a funeral bell to me.

I finish the piece slowly. My focus is shot, and I'm so disappointed in myself. If I don't get into music school, I'll be stuck delivering packages my whole life.

Music is the only thing I'm good at. It's the only option out there for me.

I'm not like the other kids trying out. If they don't get into music school, daddy will send them to law school instead. I don't have rich parents. I've gotten this far on my own by sheer determination. No pushy parents to make me practice.

While the other kids in my neighborhood were hanging out at the mall, learning to smoke and flirting with boys, I was sneaking into the school music hall to play on the old piano they kept in the corner.

I trawled the internet for free piano tutorials to teach myself, and when I'd exhausted those, I begged Mom for lessons. She put in extra shifts at the factory so she was able to send me to a local teacher.

Mrs. Hays was amazing. She never seemed to notice the over-sized, hand-me-down clothes I wore, or how much thinner I was than the other kids. She encouraged me to keep playing and practice at every opportunity. I think she knew I broke into the school music hall, but she never told anyone.

As soon as I was old enough, I got an after-school job and saved up for a secondhand piano. Mom gave her collection of Mills and Boon paperbacks to the secondhand shop and got rid of the bookcase so we could squeeze the piano into the living room. The stool was hard up against the back of the sofa, but I didn't care. I practiced every night.

Mrs. Hays told me about the Sunset Coast Music School, and how she thought I could be good enough to be a concert pianist. But I need the training first.

For the last three years that's been my focus. I should have auditioned last year, but Mom got sick and couldn't work. All those years at the factory have done something to her lungs. I had to get a job and look after her.

I kept playing though. Mrs. Hays helped me find out about scholarship programs, and this year I think I've got a shot at it. I've been putting a bit of money aside, so I'll only have to do a couple of shifts a week while I'm studying.

It'll be hard, and the other students won't be working while they study. But Mrs. Hays has shown me that I can do anything if I work hard enough, and I'm almost starting to believe her.

At least if it wasn't for this damn section that keeps tripping me up. I come out of my daydream and realize I'm still playing. The muscle memory in my hands means I can skip over the easy bits without thinking too much about it. I finish the piece and rest my hands in my lap.

Clap, clap, clap.

I spin around at the noise to find a man leaning on the doorframe and watching me. He's tall and well-built, his tight black t-shirt showcasing his bulging biceps as he claps slowly. The ink of a tattoo snakes out from under the fabric on his right arm. He's dressed all in black, with tight black jeans and even black socks.

His appearance is at odds with the elegance of the house, and I wonder for a moment if he's an employee here. But the way he's smirking at me and the casualness of his sock-covered feet make me think he may just be the owner. He definitely looks like the owner of the black convertible outside, which means he's probably Mr. Miller who owns the house and who I'm supposed to be delivering a package to.

Oh crap. I've been busted breaking and entering by the hottest man I've ever seen.

2
AYDEN

I watch the woman squirm on the piano stool. Her blonde hair is pulled into a high ponytail and wisps of it have broken free. Some strands are plastered to her face by sweat from the intensity of her playing.

The sensual notes of her music reached me in the garden where I was working and the closer I came to the music the more I craved it. I crept slowly through the house so as not to disturb the player.

I found the woman in my entranceway, concentrating and passionate. Her back ramrod straight with a pale semi-circle of skin exposed at the top of her t-shirt. Watching her from behind I was intrigued by this stranger in my house making beautiful music. Then she turned around, and she took my breath away.

Her eyes are the palest blue I've ever seen. Her cheeks are flushed from the exertion of playing, and her full pink lips form a surprised O that causes a stirring in my pants. Her t-shirt is too small, accentuating her curvy figure and a chest that's bursting out of the fabric trying to contain it.

I finish my slow clap and watch a blush spread up her neck.

"The door was open." She stands up too quickly and knocks her knee against the piano. "I've got a delivery for you." She picks a package up off the floor, her movements quick, like a sparrow. "For Mr. Miller. Is that you?"

I take the package from her, letting my finger brush against her hand. A current of energy jumps from her, sending a rush of heat shooting through my body.

"Do all delivery drivers make a habit of breaking into people's homes?"

Her face falls, and I immediately regret my harsh tone.

"I-I-I'm sorry. I rang the bell, and the door was open. I don't usually do this. Please don't report me. I'll do anything you want, just don't report me."

My member throbs at the words, and I have an image of her down on her knees. I shake the thought out of my head. I'm not an animal and this sweet woman looks too innocent for that fantasy.

I regard her for a long moment taking in the too-tight t-shirt, the worn sneakers and the youthful face, make-up free. I wonder what her story is. Why someone with such an obvious talent is delivering packages and what Gods were smiling on me to bring her into my home.

"Play for me," Her eyebrows go up in surprise.

"Play for me," I repeat. "Sit back down on that piano stool and play me a tune."

The woman looks confused and a pretty pink blush stains her cheeks. "But I..."

"You broke into my house; you touched my property. I won't call the police if you sit down and play for me."

She looks confused and I keep my expression blank. The woman turns around and sits back down on the stool.

I can sense the nervous energy running through her. I have no intention of calling the police, but I'm not going to let her know that. I have no intention of letting her out of my house just yet either. She's come in here uninvited, and she must pay the price.

"What would you like me to play?" her voice is firm, not betraying any of the nervousness her quick movements are giving away.

"Beethoven. The Moonlight Sonata. Do you know it?"

She nods and turns back to the piano. Her hair swishes, the ponytail trailing down her back. I wonder what it would be like to run my hands through it.

It's a hard piece, but she doesn't hesitate. The notes peel off the piano as her fingers glide over the keys. It starts slow and she leans in, her hair falling over her shoulder. She's good, really good. The music flows from under her fingers, the melody dancing off the keys and around the room. I lean against the door frame and watch her.

She's small but her back is ramrod straight, like she's made of steel on the inside. She seems lost in the music, oblivious of her surroundings. It's not hard to understand why she came in here. A girl with that talent shouldn't be stuck delivering packages, when she saw the piano it must have been too tempting to resist.

The shrill tones of a phone break into the music. Her fingers lift off the keys and the sudden loss of the music feels like a bandage being ripped off.

"Sorry," she mutters, reaching into her pocket.

"Hello?" she says into the phone. "Yup, I got a bit lost. Just making the delivery now. Uh-huh...yup...thanks for checking." She hangs up her phone and gets up off the stool.

"If I take too long between deliveries, they check up on me. Supposedly for my safety, but whatever." She picks up the package scanner from the floor and holds it out to me. "I need a signature."

I scribble my name in the screen for her. She's so close I can smell her scent, cardboard boxes and notes of a floral soap. Clean and good. I glance up at her and she's watching me with her pale blue eyes, like the promise of a summer day.

My heart thumps against my chest and a peculiar feeling rattles through my insides.

Mine

The word comes into my head and I know I have to have this woman.

I act on instinct, shooting my arm out and grabbing her wrist. There's a sharp intake of breath, and her sky-blue eyes widen in surprise. Her skin is soft and warm and her pulse flutters under my fingertips. I grip her wrist too tight, not wanting to let her go and she offers no resistance.

"Don't go wandering into strangers' houses. It could be dangerous."

Her eyes go even wider and her lips part. It's only an instant, but it causes the blood to rush south. She's the most beautiful woman I've ever seen and my body's reacting to her like I'm a teenage boy.

"Don't leave your door open." Her voice is husky and does nothing to help the reaction my body's having to her. "You don't know who might wander in."

I release her wrist, but she doesn't move away. I'm sure she must hear the thumping in my chest and if she looks down she'll see exactly what affect she's having on me.

The woman turns away, and before I can stop her, she darts of the open door holding her package scanner.

"Wait," I call after her but she's already running down the steps, taking them two at a time with her youthful energy. "What's your name?"

"Laila," she says, swinging door to her van open. "My name's Laila."

Laila, it's musical and suits her. But I'm not ready for her to go yet. I want to know all about Laila, I want to find out her story, where she learnt to play and why she spends her days delivering packages and not playing to sold out concert halls.

I want to run my hand through her silky hair, nibble on her soft skin and trace the lines of every curve of her body.

"I'm Ayden." I call after her.

Laila climbs into the van and slams the door closed. I feel a sense of loss as I watch her drive away. A little piece of my heart driving off with her.

Something soft circles my legs and look down to find Buddy, a stray cat I seem to have adopted and now named.

He turns his mottled grey head upwards and meows.

"I'm glad I left the door open for you." I reach down and give him a pat between the ears. He meows up at me and darts between my legs and through the door as if he owns the place. Maybe he does.

Buddy turned up the day after I moved in and wasted no time investigating the new arrival. He sauntered through the rooms as if he was familiar with the surroundings, knowing already the places where the afternoon sun fell on the floorboards.

I wonder what Buddy thinks about the empty rooms in this big house. I've only furnished two rooms: the living room which doubles as my office and a bedroom upstairs. The other rooms sit empty. Nothing, and nobody, to fill them with.

I bought the house because I like the garden, and because despite its quiet location, the internet speed is fast. Which means I can sit anywhere within the grounds and work if I want.

I follow Buddy distractedly, thinking about Laila and her bright eyes and full lips and the raw talent of her playing. I retrieve my laptop and open a web browser. I know what I have to do to see her again.

3
LAILA

*H*oly hell! My heart is racing as I pull out of the driveway. Ayden's got to be the hottest man I've ever laid eyes on, and my body knows it too. My heart's working overtime, my cheeks are flushed, and there's a dampness in my panties from the wet heat he seems to have caused down there.

I'm so flustered that I miss my turn-off and have to double back to get onto the main highway. I inhale deeply and tell myself to calm down. It's two days before the audition for music school. Really not the time to lose it just because I met a hot guy.

I drum my fingers on the steering wheel and try to pick up the rhythm, but I keep thinking about the current of electricity that passed through me when we touched. Did he feel it too?

I let out an exasperated sigh. What does it matter? I'll never see him again anyway. Unless I stalk his house because I do know where he lives. Mr. Miller.

"Laila Miller." It sounds good said out loud.

I laugh at my own ridiculousness. Even if I did see him again, what would a good-looking, obviously rich and successful guy like that want with a girl like me?

I wake up early the next morning like I do every morning and sit down at the piano to start my scales. The keys feel heavy compared to the baby grand, or maybe it's my fingers that are heavy and tired from a restless night. I didn't sleep well.

My head was full of thoughts of Ayden, and my body wouldn't relax. It was feverish with heat, craving his touch. The touch of a man I only met for five minutes.

My fingers drag over the keys, and I can't seem to move them any faster. My timing is all over the place, and after too many wrong notes I give up.

Mrs. Hays taught me that sometimes it's better to walk away for a while than to force it. But the audition is tomorrow, so there's not a lot of time to get it right.

I'll go into work early, I decide. Then I can finish early and get some good solid practice in tonight.

I'm back at the depot loading up for the lunch run when I see the packages. There's a stack of them. Wrapped in brown paper and all addressed to Mr. Miller.

My heart flutters in my chest. I put them in the

back of the van and swing into the driver's seat. I check my hair in the rearview mirror and head off.

Ten minutes later I'm pulling into the long driveway of Ayden Miller. My heart beats faster as the house comes into view. I pull up and start unloading the packages from the back of the van.

The door is open again and I ring the bell, my stomach doing little flips. This time he appears quickly, and I wonder if he's been waiting. The thought makes my stomach flip-flop again.

My breath catches in my throat at the site of Ayden. His dark hair is ruffled and he's wearing a tight black t-shirt again, showing off his toned arms and the intriguing tattoo.

"You've got another delivery," I say. "Actually, there's a few." I place the packages by the door. "I'll just get the others."

I turn to head back to the van but he reaches out and grabs my wrist. "Don't bother."

His touch is electric, and it sends a shock of heat through my body and makes the place between my legs tingle.

"Come inside and play." He leads me into the house and toward the piano, not letting my arm go until I'm seated on the stool.

I'm on fire just being near this man, and I wonder if he feels it too.

I start to play. The notes flow easily, my fingers light over the keys. I feel a weight inside me lift, and I realize how worried I'd been by this morning's shoddy practice.

I'm aware of Ayden watching me and it sends a thrill down into my fingers, making them dance over the keys. I close my eyes and lose myself in the music.

When I get to the end of the piece, he's standing next to me. I'm eye level with his belt, and I can see the outline of his erection. A rush of heat goes through my body knowing that my playing is having an effect on this man.

He crouches down so he's at eye level with me. "That was beautiful."

All I can do is nod. He's so close I can smell his aftershave. The tempo of my heart's pounding in my chest.

"You're talented."

He reaches out a hand and tilts my chin toward him. I part my lips as his mouth crashes into mine. My lips tingle with desire, sending a thrill coursing through my body.

I'm kissing a complete stranger and I should push him away and run out of here, but I don't. It feels too good to kiss him, it feels right and beautiful and as natural as the music I've just been playing. So I don't push him away, instead I turn myself toward Ayden, wanting more.

His hand runs down my neck and over my breasts causing delicious shivers to course through my body. He pulls at the bottom of my t-shirt, and we break apart so he can pull it over my head.

The cool air makes my skin shiver in anticipation. Then his warm hands are on me, running over my body and cupping my breasts. His hand slides around to unhook my bra, letting my breasts fall free. I hear an intake of breath.

"You're beautiful."

He sits back on his haunches, his eyes roaming over my body. My nipples harden under his gaze. I barely know him, but it feels so right to let him look at me. I want him to see all of me. He stands up slowly, and when he speaks his voice is husky.

"Play for me, Laila."

The words send a thrill deep into my core. He's opened up something inside of me. I want to play for him, and I want to do dirty things to him, and a piece of my heart might just be falling for him.

"What do you want to hear?"

"Anything, anything you want."

I start to play. My body feels free, and the music flows with a freedom I've never felt before. I'm aware of him beside me watching my naked skin, my breasts swaying with the music, and it adds a tension and anticipation.

My breathing becomes heavy as I play and as the music builds. He undoes his belt beside me. I'm pulled so tight every note builds with anticipation, dripping with desire.

Out of the corner of my eye, I see him reach into his pants and ease out his hard member. It's thick and long, and I almost drop a note stealing a glance. My pussy responds with a gush of wetness, and I trip over the notes. The clang of an unruly G flat rings out.

"Keep playing," he commands.

I focus on the piano and pick up the piece.

He runs his hand down the length of his shaft. Long deliberate pulls, and it's all I can do to concentrate on the music. My hands are flying over the keys as the crescendo builds. He moves behind me and slides a hand into my hair.

His fingers trail down my neck and slide down to my chest, feeling for the hard bud of my nipple. I'm on fire under his touch, my chest heaving as I keep playing. He presses up behind me, and I feel the hardness of his dick pushing into my shoulder blades. He moves it back and forth across my back as his hand strokes my breast.

I'm panting now, my pussy throbbing, aching for his touch. My fingers race toward the climax of the piece. He groans behind me, and I feel a drip of precum on my back. The music reaches its height and I crash through the last few notes, the passion coursing through my body finding its release in the final keys.

I play the final note, and while it's still lingering in the air, I turn on the stool to face him. His dick is hard and glistening, and without hesitation I open my lips and slide him inside.

4
AYDEN

The sudden heat of her mouth on my cock makes me cry out. She slides her lips down my shaft, and the wetness and heat make me almost lose it.

I grip her hair and pull her toward me. Her mouth glides up and down my shaft as her tongue darts out to lick my rim. My nerve endings are on fire as I thrust myself into her inviting mouth.

Her hand slides around to grasp the base. Her fingers are strong and sure, moving deftly up my shaft following the movement of her mouth.

"Touch yourself, Laila." My voice sounds croaky, and I know I'm close to release. While one hand runs teases my sensitive bits, her other hand moves down to the place between her legs.

She slides a hand into her pants and starts stroking rhythmically. The head of my cock bangs against the back of her throat, and she moans as I grip her hair and pull her toward me, making her breasts bounce up and down.

My climax builds as thunderously as the music she played. I thrust hard and release myself inside her. Hot cum hits the back of her throat, and she moans as her own orgasm courses through her.

Her mouth keeps sucking until her shuddering stops, and she's got every last drop out of me. I'm totally spent.

I slide out of her mouth, and she licks her lips. Her dreamy smile makes me start to harden again. I want to bend her over this piano stool and claim her properly. I pull her up and kiss her hard, tasting my own cum. She's wet between the legs, and I push myself against her.

Her phone rings out from her discarded bag. I grind into her, ignoring it. The phone rings again.

"That'll be the head office checking up on me."

"Leave it," I tell her. "I've got plans for you."

"I wish I could," she says, diving for the bag. "But if I don't answer it, they'll send a search party."

"Yeah, I'm here," she says into the phone. "Got held up, but I'm about to get back on the road...uh-huh...okay, thanks."

She hangs up the phone and starts dressing. I grab her wrist and bring it to my lips, kissing the delicate hairs on her arms.

"Stay."

She looks torn as she shakes her head. "I can't. I've got to work."

Laila breaks away and gathers her t-shirt. I help her shrug it on, not wanting her to leave, not like this.

"What is someone so talented doing working as a delivery girl?"

"It's a long story."

She picks up the signing screen and holds it out to me. It's so final, all business like, But this isn't where our story ends.

"Stay and tell me over dinner."

She sighs. "I can't stay. I'll get fired. And I need this job."

I scribble my signature for her but I'm not giving up on Laila.

"Quit the job. I'll look after you now."

She laughs as if I'm joking. "I might just take you up on that."

Later that evening, I've got my laptop open with Buddy sprawled on the couch next to me, peacefully sleeping like only a cat can.

A friend of mine, Alex, is spending the summer in the Bahamas, and he wants me to join him. There's a villa for rent near his right on the beach. I scroll through the photos he sent. Blue skies, deserted beaches, him drinking cocktails with two beautiful women wearing nothing but string bikinis.

This has been my life for the last several years. I run an online business that means I can work remotely from anywhere. I've employed a team who are based all over the world, and I only have to log in for a few hours every couple of days to keep the business running.

In the last five years, I've traveled all over the world, sometimes taking a hotel room for a few days, sometimes renting a place for a few months. As long as there's a good internet connection I can work.

It was wonderful at first, seeing the world and all it has to offer. I took cooking classes in Italy, learned to surf in Indonesia, and hiked the Southern Alps of New Zealand.

But I began to get weary of the traveling life. I started spending longer in places. I rented a hut on Goa Beach for three months, then a chateau in the south of France for four months. But what I was really missing was home. Or *a* home to be specific.

I came back to the States and bought this place not too far from where I grew up. I thought I wanted somewhere to settle down. Only now I'm feeling restless again. I've realized home isn't a place; it's the people who live there.

"You won't last six months," was Alex's prediction. "You'll be back on the road. It's in your blood; you're a born traveler."

He's pretty persistent about spending the summer in the Bahamas. While I'm itching to move, my heart sinks at the thought of another frivolous summer. I look at his picture again. The girls in the bikinis whose smiles are a bit too wide, their eyes a bit too hard. I snap my laptop shut, startling the cat.

"Alexa, play Beethoven's Moonlight Sonata," I instruct my voice recognition system.

I lean back and close my eyes, remembering Laila playing. Her straight back, her nimble fingers, and the way they deftly danced over my balls and dick. Her strong fingers pulling at me while her delicate mouth sucked.

I'm hard instantly from thinking about her. I pull my throbbing member out of my pants and stoke it in time to the music. I'm thinking about her mouth and her breasts, and it doesn't take long for my climax to erupt out of me. But instead of feeling satisfied I'm still thinking about Laila, aching for her. I know I won't be satisfied until I claim her properly as mine.

I get up off the couch, a restless energy coursing through me. I jog up the stairs and pace the upper hallway. The music blares out through the upstairs speakers, haunting the empty rooms.

I fling open the doors to each room I pass. The curtains are drawn, there's dust gathering on the windowsills, and spider webs forming in the corners of the walls. I wonder what this house would be like with children running through these halls. These empty rooms painted with colorful murals, bunk-beds full of soft toys and novelty pillows. A woman leaning over the bed to kiss my son goodnight.

A different ache starts to build inside of me. It's not just Laila's curvy body I crave. I want her as my woman, my wife, the mother of my children. The realization hits me like a brick. I can't explain it. I barely know her, but I know for sure she's the one for me.

I jog down the stairs and go back to my laptop. I pull up the email from Alex and write quickly, letting him know I won't be coming to the Bahamas. Then I put in the next-day delivery order that will bring Laila back to my house. That will bring Laila home.

5
LAILA

"amn." I bring my fingers to a halt on the keys, which seem to all be in the wrong order this morning.

"Try it again," Mom says patiently, "and don't swear."

She's in her bathrobe and faded pink slippers, hunched over the kitchen stove. She insisted on getting up today and making me breakfast to set me up for the audition.

I don't have the heart to tell her I don't think I can eat. My stomach's been doing double flips all night, and it's not just because of the audition.

I can't stop thinking about Ayden. His intense gaze on me, his husky voice, the taste of him in my mouth. I moved around all night, trapping myself in the bedsheets, waking up sweaty and aching.

I touched myself thinking about him, but it brought no release. It's not just his touch I crave. I feel drawn to him, like I know him already, like I've always known him. Which is ridiculous as I've only just met Ayden.

That's what comes from reading too many of Mom's Mills and Boons as a teenager. And now here I am letting fantasies about a man I barely know get in the way of the biggest audition of my life.

I take a deep breath and start again. My hand jerks out and I hit the wrong key. I come to a clanging stop, tears threatening my eyes.

"I can't do it."

"Of course you can." Mom comes over, waving the spatula at me. "You've worked hard for this. You can do it. I know you can, and I don't want to hear you speak otherwise."

I can't help smiling at her cross, no-nonsense approach. It's the same tone she's used every time I've gotten so frustrated I've wanted to give up.

"You know the piece," she says more gently. "Take some deep breaths and relax."

I stretch my hands out in front of me and close my eyes, breathing in deeply. Once my breath has settled, I open my eyes and begin to play.

I move through the piece carefully, hitting the right notes, keeping the rhythm. The notes sound different on my old piano compared to Ayden's baby grand. Suddenly thoughts of him fill my head—his smile, his scent, his taste. My hand falters, and I fumble a sequence.

"Damn, damn, damn!" I slam my fingers down on the duplicitous keys.

Mom doesn't tell me off for swearing, which means she's really worried about me. Instead she comes over and rubs my back.

"Maybe you should go back to bed." she suggests. "Get some rest and try again later."

"I need to go to work." I stand up, and she moves back to the kitchen. We both know I can't afford to miss a day of work. With some persuading I was able to schedule my audition for the end of the day, just after my shift finishes.

Mom serves up the eggs, and we eat in silence. I mostly push mine around the plate and try to take a few mouthfuls to keep her happy.

My stomach is clenched in a tight nervous ball, and it doesn't ease when I leave the house a few minutes later. The tense feeling builds throughout the day, until by the time my shift is almost over, I'm a tight ball of nervous energy.

The last delivery of the day is to Ayden's house. My heart soared when I picked up the afternoon deliveries and saw Mr. Miller and his address. It made me smile, and for just a moment the hard ball in my stomach eased a little. Then I remembered the audition and how bad I was this morning, and it tightened right back up.

Now as I pull into his house there are the familiar sounds of the crunch of the tires on gravel and the scrape of the overhanging trees on the top of the van. When the house comes into view, I feel the knot in my stomach relax a little. There's a cat sitting on the front step as if waiting for me, and the door is ajar but there's no sign of Ayden.

My heart's thumping louder than a kettle drum as I mount the stairs with my arms full of packages, briefly wondering what he's ordering but not really caring as it gives me an excuse to see him. The cat wraps itself around my legs purring, and my stomach loosens a little bit more.

"Hello?" I call as I push the door open.

He's sitting on the stairs waiting for me. My breath catches at the sight of him. His hair is shaggy like he hasn't slept, and dark stubble courses over his chin. As he stands to greet me his jeans tighten over his thighs, revealing the outline of his manly package. I almost drop the packages I'm holding. He strides over and takes them off me, discarding them on the floor.

"I've waited all day for you," he says, reaching a hand out to stroke my cheek. His touch is electric, and it shoots right through my body. But I'm so wired my head jerks away.

He drops his hand instantly. "What's up?"

"I've got this big audition, and I'm gonna mess it up," I blurt out.

Before he turns away, I see the relief on his face. Maybe he thought it was something else, could this man really feel the same about me as I do him?

"We can fix that." He reaches for my hand and leads me over to the piano stool. We sit together, and before I know it, I'm telling him all about the music school and piano lessons and the shitty practice I did this morning and how three days ago I could play fine and now I can't concentrate on the music.

He listens silently until I'm finished, until all my misgivings are laid out before him.

"Play for me now," he says. "Play the audition piece."

He shuffles over on the piano stool, giving me the space I need. I wipe my tears and turn to the piano.

I play a few scales to warm up. Ayden's so close I can smell his crisp aftershave. It's invigorating, and my fingers fly over the scales. I pause, ready to start.

"Wait," he says, leaning in so his breath tickles my neck. "Play with your top off."

It's an indecent request but I don't hesitate. I trust this man and the request makes me tingle with anticipation.

He lifts up my t-shirt and pulls it over my head. It drops to the floor beside me, and I begin to play.

As I start to play, he runs a hand up my back. I shiver beneath his warm fingers. It's electric and also comforting, and I feel the tension ease a little more.

He leans in and kisses the skin on the back of my neck. The shock of his warm breath shoots through me right down to my fingertips. They fly over the keys, confident and steady.

As I play, his hand slides around to cup my breast. The nipples instantly harden as he pinches and teases. I catch my breath. It's a delicious sensation, like I'm floating in pleasure above the waves of music.

My playing doesn't stop as he slides off the piano stool and kneels before me. His hands slide under my skirt and up my thighs. I gasp as he finds the wet fabric of my panties. Slowly, he pulls them down my thighs and hooks them off my feet.

My heart is racing, and I'm breathing hard as I play; the slow melody pings with anticipation.

Then his hand is on my thigh, pulling one leg open as he kisses the delicate skin. The sensation moves slowly up my inner thigh until he's kissing the folds of my pussy.

The music changes as the tempo picks up. His tongue darts out, matching the speed of the notes. A burst of heat and wetness flows to meet him. I lean into the music and keep playing as he strums the rhythm with his tongue.

The music is building, and I climb with it. The notes ring out urgent and fast. The heat flows up my body to my fingertips, the passion of my body riding on the notes.

He pulls me into him as the crescendo builds. My fingers fly over the keys, urgent and passionate as my climax explodes. I cry out as my body releases, and the music reaches its peak to match mine. My pussy throbs as I release the final few notes. The last chord rings out in the air as my body finishes shuddering. The tension is gone. I've played the piece perfectly. Better than perfect; I've played it with passion and purpose.

He comes out from in front of the stool and stands up.

"How long have you got before that damn phone rings?" he says, unbuckling his belt.

6
AYDEN

Hearing Laila play while I licked her was the sexiest thing I've ever done in my life. I'm hard as a rock, and if I don't claim Laila soon, I'll explode. She's looking at me with bright eyes and a sheen of sweat on her upper lip, and fuck, I have to have her.

Her phone starts to ring, and I grab it and throw it against the wall. It smashes, and her eyes go wide.

"They'll come looking for me," she says.

"And they'll find you here. Getting fucked by me." Her eyes go wide and rush of blood goes south.

She licks her lips "I'd love to, but I have to get to my audition."

"What time?" I growl.

She looks at her watch. "Thirty minutes." She jumps up, startled, and scrambles for her clothes. "It's across town. I have to go."

Fuck. I take a deep breath and call on all the restraint I have. It takes all my willpower not to convince her to stay so I can bend her over and plunge into her. But this is her big day, her big audition. I can wait for my girl a little bit longer.

"Play like you just did and you'll blow them away."

"Thank you." She smiles at me, and I pull her toward me into a kiss. Soft and slow, her lips part for me. I swallow my desire and pull away.

"You'd better get going. But come straight back here after wards."

She nods.

I watch from the doorway as she races down the steps and to her van.

"Good luck," I call as she pulls away. I watch until her van disappears down the drive.

Then I go inside and pull out my aching hard-on. I sit by the piano stool. Her scent is still on the neat velvet, and I breathe her in.

The faint smell of her pussy sends my blood racing. She's left her panties for me, and I chuckle thinking of her auditioning with a bare pussy. The thought makes my dick throb. I press her underwear to my nose and inhale deeply. It's sweet and sticky and smells like home.

With my dick in my hand and her panties to my face I take a few quick strokes, thinking about her taste and remembering the music. It doesn't take long for cum to shoot out, and I catch it in her panties.

It's a small release, and it does nothing to ease the desire burning within me. I thrust Laila's panties into my pocket and go upstairs. I'll pace the halls like an agitated animal until she comes back, and I can finally claim her as my own.

7
LAILA

I take the stone stairs two at a time. Sunset Coast Music School is emblazoned grandly across the entrance supported by two round pillars. I pause at the top of the stairs to smooth down my hair. A breeze lifts up my skirt, tickling my bare pussy and sending a shiver through my body. I smile to myself and push the door open.

I follow the signs to the auditions and get to the sign-in desk exactly on time. I give my name to the lady, and she raises an eyebrow at me.

"We have a warmup area to the left with some practice pianos." She indicates a doorway. "But you'll need to go straight in."

"It's okay," I say, flashing her a smile. "I'm already warm."

"They're waiting for you," she says sternly, and a tremor of nervousness runs through me.

I follow her to a room at the end of the corridor.

With each clack of her heels on the wooden flooring, my stomach clenches tighter. She goes ahead and announces my name to the room.

"Good afternoon," I say to the four adjudicators sitting behind the large table. There's a mumbled response, and one man puts his fist in front of his mouth as he tries to stifle a yawn.

I realize what a bad move it was asking for the last slot of the afternoon. They're done for the day and can't wait to get home.

I stand there for a moment, not sure if they're going to speak to me.

"Take a seat at the piano, dear," says a woman with a kindly smile. Her grey hair is pulled back in a loose bun. Stray wispy bits float around her head like a halo. I recognize her as the dean of the school. Her disheveled appearance masks a creative soul whose reputation for eccentricity is almost as big as her reputation for music. She's the one I need to impress.

The knot in my stomach gets tighter as I sit on the hard wooden stool.

"I'm playing Chopin."

The woman nods encouragingly. I place my fingers lightly on the keys and begin.

It's hot in the room, and the tenseness has crept back into my body. My fingers stumble, and I hit a wrong note. I'm so furious with myself that I hit another. I lift my fingers off the keys, and the music stops.

My heart is thumping in my chest, and it feels like I might throw up. One of the adjudicators coughs.

I turn to face them. The woman with the bun is writing something on her note pad, probably about how terrible I am. But the man next to her is worse. He's shuffling his papers into a neat pile, like he's done for the day and getting ready to go home.

They've written me off. All those years of hard work, and I've messed up the audition. I feel the hot sting of tears at the back of my eyes. No, I tell myself. It doesn't end like this.

"Can I start again?" I ask.

The woman looks up at me and smiles.

"Of course, dear," she says putting down her pen. "Take your time."

I take a deep breath and start again. I use the focus techniques I learned off the internet and center my mind on the music. I close my eyes, feeling my way over the notes.

A memory slides into my consciousness of Ayden's warm hand on my back, his breath tickling my neck. I smile to myself; the memory is so clear I feel the hairs on my neck rise.

I lean into the music, channeling the feeling into the notes. My stomach relaxes as my body responds to the memory of his touch. I can almost feel his hands on me, warm fingers sliding up my thigh. I part my legs slightly, and cool air caresses my naked pussy.

The music builds, and my breathing deepens. I'm

remembering his lips on my thighs, his tongue on my wet folds.

Sweat beads on my forehead as my fingers fly over the keys. My body is alive with the memory of him licking and caressing me. My fingers zing along the keys, trembling with desire and yearning. I channel my passion through the notes, and they sing out as the tempo lifts.

The crescendo starts to build as my hands dance fast and furious over the keys. I'm in a frenzy of passion as I reach the climax of the music. Thrashing out the notes, I stand up off the stool and it crashes to the floor behind me. I keep going, unable to stop until the final urgent notes of the climax of the music.

I pause, breathing hard before caressing the keys with the diminuendo. The final note of the piece rings out, and then there's silence. My chest is heaving, my panting breaths the only sound. I wipe the sweat off my face and slowly bring my focus back into the room.

There's silence from the panel. I dare not turn around to face them. I feel vulnerable and exposed. I've given them everything I have, and I knocked over their piano stool. They must think I'm crazy.

Slowly, I turn to face them. The man who was yawning is leaning forward on the table. The kindly woman is sitting bolt upright, a wide smile on her face. The others are staring at me.

"That was extraordinary." The woman beams at me. "Welcome to the Sunset Coast Music School."

"You can't just offer her a place," says one of the men. "It has to go through the board."

"I can, and I have," says the woman. She steps around the table and comes to shake my hand. "I'm Professor Chomsky," she says. "I'll be teaching you."

"Margaret," says the man. "This is most unorthodox."

She laughs. "When have you ever known me to be orthodox?" her handshake is firm, and her eyes are clear and bright.

"I'll push you hard," she says holding onto my hand. "I'll teach you technique and focus and control. But only you can bring the passion. Can you do that?"

I think of Ayden again, buried between my thighs.

"I can bring the passion," I tell her.

8
AYDEN

I'm waiting on the steps for Laila when she pulls up. Not in the delivery van this time, but in an old battered hatchback. First thing tomorrow we're going car shopping, I decide. I'll buy her something safe and reliable and stylish, of course. Any car she wants.

She throws open the car door before it's barely come to a stop. The smile on her face tells me everything I need to know.

"They offered me a place!" She leaps into my arms and I bury my face in her hair, breathing in her scent.

"I knew you could do it."

She tells me all about the audition and the immediate acceptance offer. I carry her inside as she talks. She's animated and happy and full of energy, and her body's wriggling against mine, making me hard.

I take her to the piano stool, and draw her onto my

lap. She's in the process of telling me about the music school when her face falls.

"What is it?" I ask

"I'm going to be based here for music school."

"Perfect. You can move in here with me."

"But is this your regular home?" She indicates the empty rooms leading from the entryway. "It doesn't look like you're here permanently."

I lift her chin so she's looking me in the eye.

"I want to be wherever you are. I've done a lot of traveling in the last few years, but it was all empty Laila. I never wanted to stay anywhere until I met you. You're it for me, Laila. Wherever you are, is where I'm calling home."

She smiles at me, and I know I mean it. I'll do anything to have this girl smile at me like that every day.

"And besides, there'll be holiday breaks. We can go away then. Anywhere you like. I can't wait to show you the world. But for the next four years this is home."

I lean in and kiss her mouth. Her lips part for me, and I press forward with my tongue. I slide onto the floor in front of her and run my hands up her thighs. I gasp as my fingers meet her soft pussy.

"Where are your panties?" I ask mock horrified.

"I believe they're probably in your pocket." She grins at me, and I laugh.

"Guilty."

I had forgotten she went out with no panties. The thought of her walking through town with nothing but the wind against her pussy sends a shiver of heat down to my dick. I brush her delicate lips with my fingers, and my hard-on intensifies. I have to have her now.

I pull her off the piano stool and onto my lap. Her skirt flies up, and I catch a glimpse of glistening pink before it settles over her again.

I press my mouth against her as my hand scrambles for my belt buckle. She matches my urgency, and her strong hands come around and release me from my pants. Her warm hands wrap around me, sending pinpricks of heat through my nerve endings. Her hands are firm and hot, but it's not enough. I can smell her pussy, and I want to be inside her.

"I need to fuck you now," I tell her as I take my dick out of her hands. I grab a condom from my pocket and rip it open with my teeth.

Her hand comes out to stop me as I place it over my tip.

"I want to feel all of you," she says.

My blood gushes at the prospect of going in skin against skin. I think of the image I had yesterday of children running through these empty halls. Then I think of how hard she's worked to get into music school. I can't let her give that up. We have the rest of our lives together, plenty of time to start a family.

"I want that too, but only after you've finished your training. You're too talented."

She takes the base of my cock in her hands. "Thank you for thinking of me. But I'm on the pill."

Laila gives me a wicked grin and I toss the condom away. "In that case…"

I lift her skirt and rub my tip against the soft pink folds of her. She moans as my dick passes over her clit. She's wet and ready, but I make myself hold off a little longer just to be sure. She presses her thighs against me and leans back onto the piano stool. I rub against her a few times, then gently slide the tip into her wet opening. She sits up, her eyes wide.

"You okay?" I ask.

"Yeah. It's just so big."

I chuckle. "That's only the tip, baby."

"I've never done this before."

Holy shit, she's a virgin. No wonder she's so tight. The blood is thundering in my ears. I'm going to claim her for the first time and for the only time. She's all mine.

"It's going to hurt a little, babydoll. It'll hurt when I break through your virgin barrier."

Saying it out loud makes my dick shudder in anticipation. I lift her up and slide her pussy further down my tip.

"Oh my God," she whispers, her eyes wide.

I hold her there, letting her get used to my girth. My thumb reaches round to rub her clit in soft circles until her eyes close and she moans in pleasure. I pull her down a little further on my impatient cock. It's so fucking tight and she cries out, her eyes flying open. My dick's resting against her hymen, and it's taking everything I've got not to slam her down onto my lap and thrust deep inside her. Instead I keep rubbing with my thumb as I slide her up and down the top of my shaft.

"You okay, babydoll?"

"Y-yes," she whimpers. "It feels so good."

Her clit's hard under my touch and I move my thumb a little faster, matching her breathing. Her climax is building, and my dick is pulsing under the restraint.

"Come for me, babydoll."

She cries out as her body releases wetness over my dick. As she loses control, I maintain mine, pressing my thumb against her as I hold her on the end of my dick.

Her pussy pulses, contracting my cock into a delicious tightness. I wait until her shuddering stops, and then I start rubbing her slit again. She's leaning back, her eyes closed and her thighs twisting into me. It's the sexist sight I've ever seen.

She moans in pleasure, and I can sense another orgasm is building. She opens her eyes; they're full of need as she locks on mine.

"I want all of you," she says. "Put it all in me."

"You ready for me, babydoll?"

She nods. I press my thumb against her clit, and as the climax is about to take her, I pull her down my shaft.

"Fuuuck!" she cries as wet, tight pussy envelopes my dick. Her pussy's contracting with the orgasm and the tightness, and the heat and her pleasure causes an instant explosion. My cry matches hers as we lock together, clinging on to each other, our pleasure running together.

As the shuddering stops, I plant kisses on her head. She tastes salty from the exertion, and sweet.

She opens her eyes and looks at me all dreamy and satisfied. "Can we do it again?" she asks.

"Babydoll, we can do it every day for the rest of our lives if you want."

She throws her arms around me, and my heart melts into her.

"That sounds perfect," she says.

Something brushes against my leg, and Buddy jumps up on the piano stool.

"Hope you don't mind us sticking around," I say. He lies down on the stool, and his purr echoes around the room.

"Looks like we all found a home," I say.

EPILOGUE

LAILA

Six years later...

There's a harsh rap on the door. "Five minutes, Mrs. Miller."

"She's almost ready," my husband calls.

He looks back at me, mischief in his eyes, and we giggle like naughty school children. Ayden winks at me, then dives his head back under my skirt. His tongue runs over my pink folds and pleasure courses through me, escaping as a moan from my parted lips.

He picks up the pace, his tongue lapping against my clit. I lean back on the dressing table and open my legs, opening myself up to him. His finger slides inside, and I cry out as he plunges deeper, creating a delicious pressure against my clit.

The door handle rattles, and the irate stage manager calls again. "Curtain opens in two minutes. We need you onstage now!"

"I'm coming!" I cry breathlessly, which makes my husband chuckle into my pussy. The hot breath and the vibrations of his laughter send me over the edge, and I push myself into him as I reach my climax.

It courses through me with the power of a full orchestra reaching the crescendo. I grip the sides of the dressing table and cry out until my body stops shaking.

I'm still throbbing with ecstasy as I pull up my panties and smooth down my hair. My face is slightly red, but I'm buzzing, and I'm ready.

We're halfway through my second world tour as a solo pianist. With Ayden's support and Professor Chomsky's strict practice regime, I finished my training in just three years. I've been touring ever since.

At almost every stop, my husband has some favorite haunt or local treasure to show me. But my favorite stops are when we visit somewhere he hasn't been before. Then we get to explore it together.

It's been an amazing few years of performing and traveling, and only stopping to have our two children. They come with us wherever we go.

The oldest is three years old now, and already he's been to more cities then most people will ever visit. We always come back to our home though.

Buddy will be waiting for us on the steps. Mom will have aired it out for us, and she'll stay for a few days playing with the children in the garden.

I love performing. The critics say I have a raw, powerful energy, as if there's some secret force inside of me. It's no secret really. My husband fires my desire and sends me onstage dripping with passion and love.

When I play, I remember that first time he made love to me, and all our lust and love and passion for each other comes out in the music.

It's even more potent when I'm pregnant, my body ripe and full of hormones, like it is tonight. Ayden doesn't know it yet, but I took a test this morning and child number three will be joining us soon.

I'll tell him tonight after the show when we go back to the hotel. After we check on our sleeping babies, he'll run me a bubble bath. I always like a soak after a performance to unwind. He usually joins me, and we'll talk about our day and what we want to see in Verona tomorrow before we move on to the next stop on the tour.

We've got three more stops left, and then we're back home for a while.

I open the dressing room door and surprise the flustered stage manager bending down to knock

"I'm ready," I tell him.

My husband walks with me to the stage. He'll sit in the wings and watch the performance. I like knowing he's there. And he's never missed a show.

The lights in the auditorium go dim, and the chatter from the audience dies instantly. It's a full house. The MC goes onto the stage, and I feel my stomach tighten with nerves. I don't understand the Italian, but I hear my name as I'm announced.

He holds out a hand indicating my entrance. I look over to Ayden, and he gives me a reassuring nod.

He's in his trademark tight black t-shirt; he could be one of the stagehands, only sexier. His arms bulge out of the sleeves, and a memory floods my consciousness. His arms holding me tight, balancing me above his cock as he thrusts me down his shaft and onto his lap.

As if reading my thoughts, he throws me a mischievous grin and licks his lips, which are still glistening from our escapades in the dressing room. My pussy contracts with the memory, and the knot in my stomach melts away.

I take a deep breath and walk onstage.

WHAT TO READ NEXT

MAN OF STRENGTH

An undercover billionaire and a curvy girl on the run…

Tyler

We're losing money at the fitness club, and I've gone undercover to find out what's going on. Then I meet Zoe. From the moment she walks in on me in the gym showers, I know I need to have this woman. She's gorgeous, she's defiant, and I'm pretty sure she's hiding something.

Zoe

There's a reason I work out every day, a reason I've learned to defend myself and run fast, and a reason why I never stay in one place for long. Then I meet the hot new personal trainer at the gym, and suddenly I don't want to run anymore. But will he still want me when he learns the truth?

Man of Strength is a short and steamy age gap romance featuring a secret billionaire and a younger innocent woman.

GET YOUR FREE BOOK

Sign up to the Sadie King mailing list for a FREE book!

Fox in the Garden is an age gap steamy romance featuring an OTT billionaire and the younger woman he claims as his own.

It's a bonus book in the Filthy Rich Love series, exclusive to my email subscribers.

Sign up here:
authorsadieking.com/bonus-scenes

If you're already a subscriber check your latest email for the link that will take you to all the bonus content.

BOOKS & SERIES BY SADIE KING

Sunset Coast

Underground Crows MC

Short and steamy MC romance stories of obsessed men and curvy girls.

Sunset Security

A security firm run by ex-military men who become obsessed with their curvy girls.

Filthy Rich Love

The billionaires of the Sunset Coast. These alpha men fall hard and fall fast for the younger curvy women who crash into their world.

Men of the Sea

Super short and steamy tales from Temptation Bay of bad boys and curvy girls.

Love and Obsession

A bad boy trilogy featuring a thief, a henchman and an ex-military hitman who finds redemption with his curvy girl.

Wild Heart Mountain

Military Heroes

Kobe brings together a group of military veterans who live on the side of Wild Heart Mountain. Can these wounded warriors find love or do their scars cut too deep?

Wild Riders MC

This group of ex-military bikers fall hard and fall fast when they encounter the curvy women who heal their hearts.

Mountain Heroes

Steamy stories featuring the men and women from Wild Heart Mountain's Search and Rescue and Fire service.

Temptation

A damaged hero and a lost virgin in an explosive instalove retelling of the Hansel and Gretel story set in the woods of Wild Heart Mountain.

A Runaway Bride for Christmas

A snowstorm keeps this runaway bride trapped in the cabin of the mountain's biggest grump.

A Secret Baby for Christmas

Mr. Porter's Christmas takes a surprise turn when his daughter's best friend turns up with his baby.

Maple Springs

Small Town Sisters

Five curvy sister's inherit a dog hotel. But can they find love? Short and steamy instalove romance!

Candy's Café

A small-town cafe that's all heart. Meet the sister's who run it and the customer's who keep coming back.

All the Single Dads

These single dad hotties are fiercely protective and will do anything for the ones they love.

Men of Maple Mountain

These men are OTT possessive and will stop at nothing to claim the curvy innocent women they become obsessed with.

The Carter Family

Blue collar men find love with curvy girls in these quick read instalove romances.

Curvy Girls Can

Short, sweet and steamy instalove stories about sassy curvy women and the men who love them.

The Seal's Obsession

A soft stalker, secret baby, military romance. Featuring an OTT obsessed alpha male and a sassy curvy girl.

Kings County

Kings of Fire

Smoking hot tales of insta-love, featuring brave heroes and sassy heroines that will melt your heart.

King's Cops

Do you love police romance books? Then the King's Cops series is for you! Short, sweet and steamy tales of insta-love, featuring brave heroes and sassy heroines that will melt your heart.

For a full list of Sadie King's books check out her website

www.authorsadieking.com

ABOUT THE AUTHOR

Sadie King is a USA Today Best Selling Author of over 120 short and steamy contemporary romances. She loves writing about military heroes and the sassy women who heal their hearts.

Sadie lives in New Zealand with her ex-military husband and raucous young son.

When she's not writing she loves catching waves with her son, running along the beach, and drinking good wine, preferably with a book in hand.

www.authorsadieking.com

THANK YOU

Thank you for reading my story! If you enjoyed it, please consider leaving a review, they mean so much to authors and it helps other readers find books they might like.

                Thank you!
                Sadie xx

Milton Keynes UK
Ingram Content Group UK Ltd.
UKHW041822131124
451149UK00001B/19